Win or Lose

Adapted by Heather Alexander

Based on the series created by Michael Poryes and Rich Correll & Barry O'Brien

Part One is based on the episode, "Money For Nothing, Guilt For Free," Written by Heather Wordham

Part Two is based on the episode, "Debt It Be," Written by Sally Lapiduss and Heather Wordham

Bath · New York · Singapore · Hong Kong · Cologne · Delhi · Melbourne

First published by Parragon in 2009
Parragon
Queen Street House
4 Queen Street
Bath BA1 1HE, UK

ISBN 978-1-4075-4626-1

Printed in the UK by CPI Bookmarque, Croydon, CR0 4TD

PART ONE

Chapter One

Miley Stewart slid into her seat behind her best friend, Lilly Truscott. She glanced up at the school clock. Four more hours to go – two hundred and forty minutes.

Miley couldn't wait for school to be over that day. She and Lilly were planning to do some serious shopping that afternoon.

"Okay, I want everyone to close your eyes and find your happy place," said Miley's teacher, Mr Corelli. He nodded his head enthusiastically.

Miley glanced around the room. All her classmates had shut their eyes. She shrugged and figured she'd log some beauty *z*'s, too. She closed her eyes.

"Now imagine all the good things in your life," Mr Corelli continued.

That was easy! Miley thought of hanging out with her friends at the beach, playing the guitar, and singing in front of a cheering crowd as pop star Hannah Montana.

Miley smiled to herself. The kids at school would flip if they ever found out that teen music sensation Hannah Montana was really Miley in disguise. Only her family and best friends were in on her secret.

"Great shoes, perfect hair," Ashley Dewitt crooned. Miley frowned. There was no mistaking that annoying voice.

"Very Berry lip shine!" cried Amber Addison, Ashley's best friend.

"Oooo!" the two girls squealed.

Miley didn't have to open her eyes to know what would happen next. The two girls reached across the aisle and touched pointer fingers. *"Ssss!"* they hissed, as if they were burning hot.

"Wow!" Lilly whispered to Miley. "Even though I can't see it, it's still annoying."

Miley kept her eyes closed and nodded. "I know. Now it's in *my* happy place."

"Okay, open your eyes," her teacher instructed.

Miley looked at Mr Corelli. Today he was wearing a red cardie and, of course, a bow tie. Her teacher wore a bow tie every day.

"Now that you've had time to think about what you have, it's time to think about those who aren't as lucky," said Mr Corelli. "Yes, it's that time again for our school to raise money for . . ." He faked a drumroll. ". . . the United People's Relief fund. And you, my little relievers, are going to help the less fortunate."

"Like Ms Dawson, the librarian?" Miley's other best friend, Oliver Oken, called from the desk right behind her.

"Ms Dawson is not less fortunate. She chooses to dress that way. It's too bad," Mr Corelli said dreamily. "She could be all that and a bowl of pudding."

Just then, the classroom door opened, and Miley's classmate Sarah rushed in.

"I'm sorry I'm late, Mr Corelli," she said, out of breath. She pushed up her glasses. "I was on my way to school when I had to wrestle a cat away from a baby bird, and then I felt sorry for the cat, so I went to the pet store to get him some food, and then I saw this lost dog with a sore paw – "

Mr Corelli held up his hands, as if in surrender. "Whoa, Sarah!"

Miley had known Sarah for years, and she was always doing something to help others.

Mr Corelli looked at Sarah and sighed. "Why is it every time I talk to you I get the urge to give blood and call my mum? Which, if you knew my mum, is sort of the same thing." He pointed Sarah toward her desk. "I'm sorry," he said to the class. "Where were we?"

"You were crushing on Ms Dawson," Miley called out helpfully.

"Ewww!" Lilly said.

"No, I wasn't," Mr Corelli corrected Miley. "I was thinking about pudding." His stomach growled loudly. "Moving on.

United People's Relief. Like last year, the person or team that raises the most cha-ching gets the day off from school, their picture in the newspaper, and a three-hundred-dollar gift card to the Malibu Mall – "

The school bell rang loudly. Kids leaped out of their chairs and headed toward the door. Mr Corelli didn't mind. "Finally! Lunchtime!" he cried.

Lilly turned toward Miley. "We have to win. I need a new deck for my skateboard."

"I just want to win so Amber and Ashley don't. Otherwise it's going to be another year of listening to them gloat." Miley wrinkled her nose. Amber and Ashley had won last year, and they were *still* reminding everyone at school.

"Hey, guys," Amber said. She and Ashley stopped at Miley's and Lilly's desks.

"We know we gloated last year, and we feel really bad about that."

"So we just wanted to say good luck," Ashley added, as she patted Miley on the back. Amber nodded and patted Lilly on the back. "May the best fund-raiser win," Ashley continued. Then she and Amber skipped out the door.

"Okay, something doesn't smell right here," Miley announced.

Lilly grimaced. "Sorry. I knew I should-n't have had that breakfast burrito."

"No, I'm talking about Amber and Ashley. They're up to something, and we just have to watch our backs."

"You got it," Lilly said. She followed her friend out of the classroom.

Between classes, the halls of Seaview were like the mall the day before Christmas – packed. Some kids pushed and shoved to get to their lockers. Some walked by in an

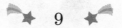

9

aimless daze. Today, Miley noticed, people were whispering even more than usual.

❀ ❀ ❀

Throughout the day, the whispering seemed to grow louder whenever Miley and Lilly walked by. Am I imagining this? Miley wondered.

As Miley and Lilly headed toward their lockers after class six, Miley was sure she heard laughter.

She whipped her head to the right. A group of girls looked innocently at her. To Miley, it looked as if they were about to start giggling.

Miley twisted the dial on her lock, and the whispers and snickers started up again. She and Lilly both spun around. The halls immediately went silent. Miley looked at the kids' faces, trying to figure out the joke. But all she got were blank stares.

Miley turned back to her locker. The laughter and mumbling grew louder. Miley could sense everyone watching her. There was no denying it. Everyone was talking about her and Lilly. But why?

She whirled around again. Suddenly her classmates were busy shuffling their notebooks or tying their sneakers. Miley couldn't take it any longer. "Okay, this has been going on for two hours. What gives, people?"

A group of seventh-grade boys shrugged their shoulders. Miley wasn't buying their innocent routine. Before she could investigate, Amber and Ashley strutted by.

"Hi, Miley," Amber called sweetly.

"Hi, Lilly," Ashley added. She turned to Amber and giggled. Then they sashayed down the hall.

Lilly frowned. "Okay, this has Amber and Ashley written all over it."

Just then, Oliver walked up to them and reached over their shoulders. "Actually," he said, pulling pieces of paper off their backs, "it has 'Dork' and 'Dorkier' written all over it."

Miley grabbed the handmade signs she and Lilly had been unaware they were wearing and ripped them to shreds. "That's it! They are going to pay for this!" She stomped down the hall. Lilly and Oliver hurried to catch up.

"Wait, wait," Lilly cried. "Was I 'Dork' or 'Dorkier'?"

Miley shot her friend a look of disbelief.

"It's important to me," Lilly explained.

"What's important is not letting Amber and Ashley win that charity drive again. I'm sick of seeing their snobby faces everywhere I turn." Miley turned the corner toward the school trophy case and jumped back in shock. "*Ahhh!*" A huge photo of

Amber and Ashley holding last year's gift card was in the front of the case.

"Well, just don't look there," suggested Lilly. She gently turned Miley around.

"*Ahhh!*" Miley shrieked again. The real Amber and Ashley stood in front of her. They held a giant-size version of this year's gift card.

"Check it out, losers," Amber taunted.

"This is as close as you'll ever get to one of these," Ashley said. Then she and Amber walked away.

Miley turned to Lilly. "We'll see about that. We'll knock on every door until our knuckles bleed," she vowed. "We'll beg and we'll plead, and we won't take 'no' for an answer!"

Lilly looked at her best friend doubtfully, but Miley was determined. It was up to them to bring down the reigning queens of mean!

Chapter Two

The sun was setting over the Malibu coast, and Miley was beyond tired. Her legs were tired, her feet were tired — even her toenails were tired. She plopped down onto the curb alongside Lilly and Oliver. Oliver shook their United People's Relief collection can. Not a sound. It was empty.

Miley replayed the afternoon in her mind. Instead of going to the mall, she and her friends had hit the streets. They had knocked on doors and rang doorbells. Every time, they heard the same thing: "No!" Then the door would slam shut.

It had been a rough afternoon, but Miley refused to give up. "Okay, I think it's time to kick it up a notch!" she told her friends. They reached out and stacked their hands one on top of the other, then raised them in a cheer. "One, two, three, let's bring the cha-ching!" they shouted together.

They rallied. At one house, Lilly and Oliver attempted to juggle while Miley spun a plate on a stick. "Hi, we're juggling for charity," Miley announced.

Slam! The door swung shut.

At the next house, the three friends tried some good old-fashioned Tennessee music. Lilly played the washboard, Oliver whistled on a jug, and Miley plucked a banjo.

"Howdy, y'all!" Miley said when a man answered the door. "We're pluckin' for charity!"

It didn't take the man long to decide what to do. *Slam!* Another door had closed and Miley, Lilly, and Oliver still hadn't collected any donations.

Then Miley remembered something. People were always more generous during the holidays. Miley and her friends bundled up in winter parkas and red elf hats. When an elderly woman answered the door at the next house, Oliver tossed some fake snow into the air. Then he and the girls launched into "The Twelve Days of Christmas."

They finished the song in a glorious three-part harmony. Even the most cold-hearted person would donate money now, Miley thought.

"Merry Christmas and don't forget the less fortunate!" she cried.

"Christmas?" The old woman looked extremely confused. "Last time I dozed off it was September. The grandkids will be here any minute. I've got to get those elves out of the attic."

"But – " Miley said, holding out the empty can.

The door slammed. The woman was gone. And so were their chances of raising any money that day.

Meanwhile, at Miley's beachside home in Malibu, her older brother, Jackson, was finishing a game of one-on-one basketball with their dad. Jackson's best friend, Cooper, watched from the sidelines.

Jackson kept his eyes on the hoop. He faked to the right, faked to the left, and dribbled down the court. His eyes still on the ball, he never saw his father take a step to the side. All Jackson saw was the orange ball twirl around the rim and drop into the basket. Score!

"Good game, son," Mr Stewart said, patting him on the back. "I almost didn't score a point."

"Don't feel bad, Dad," Jackson said, grinning. He pushed his brown hair off his sweaty forehead. "One of these days you'll finally win one."

Cooper started laughing. "If he wanted to he could win them all, fool. He's just playin' you."

Jackson was confused. "Why would he do that?"

"He feels sorry for you," Cooper explained. "I mean, look at you. For a basketball player, you're a short little fella."

"Dad, is that true?" Jackson demanded, not wanting to believe his friend. "You've been letting me win?"

"Of course not, son," Mr Stewart fibbed. "I think you're really, really good." Then, without Jackson seeing, Mr Stewart quickly motioned to Cooper to cut it out. But he wasn't quick enough.

"Wh-wh-what is all that?" Jackson asked, pointing to his father's hand, still in mid-motion.

Mr Stewart played it off by fanning himself. "I'm just cooling myself off after a brutal beating."

"It is a tad humid today," Cooper chimed in. He also waved his hand like a fan.

Jackson wasn't going to be fooled again. "Yeah, yeah, nice try. But I know what that means." He turned to his father. "I want you to stand in front of the basket and *try* this time."

"Jackson, I'm a little tired," Mr Stewart said.

"Dad, please," Jackson begged. "I have to know."

"Okay, but just remember, you asked for it." Mr Stewart stood in front of the basket. He raised his arms.

Jackson dribbled, aimed, and shot the ball. His dad effortlessly swatted it away as soon as the shot was taken.

Jackson ran down the ball before it went out of bounds. "All right," he said. "Let's see what you've got down low, Oldylocks!" Jackson dribbled quickly to the left and faked right. He raced in for the layup and – *No!* His dad easily deflected the ball.

Jackson sighed. "Oh, man, he was right! You let me win." He thought back to all the years of one-on-one basketball he had played with his dad. "Wait a minute. Do you *always* let me win?"

"I'm sorry, son. It's just that I love seeing how happy you get when you win," said Mr Stewart. "Plus, when you lose, you always make that little pouty face."

Jackson stuck his lip out and cast down his eyes. "I do not."

Cooper patted Jackson's face. "*Whoomp!* There it is."

"Well, this ends now," Jackson said. "I'm gonna beat you at something, Dad. And I am gonna beat you *so* bad."

Mr Stewart shook his head, looking exasperated. "Son, you've got your health. You've got a nice car. Why go looking for unhappiness?"

Jackson bent his arms, tucked them at his sides, and strutted around the driveway, clucking like a chicken.

"Okay, that does it," Mr Stewart said, rising to the challenge. "Name your game."

Jackson grabbed his father's hand. "One, two, three, four, I declare a thumb war."

It took about two seconds for Mr Stewart to pin Jackson's thumb under his own. Jackson fell to his knees in pain. "Ow, ow, ow, ow, *ow*!"

"It's okay, son, it's not your fault." Mr Stewart released his son's thumb. "You've got your mom's thumbs."

Jackson squealed in horror. "I have girl thumbs!"

The next afternoon in Mr Corelli's class, it was time to tally up the money that had been raised so far. Miley waited on line with her classmates. Everyone was eager to see how much money others had collected.

Miley suspected that humiliation was on the day's agenda.

Miley watched as a boy named Tyler handed Mr Corelli a fat envelope. Mr Corelli ruffled through the stack of bills and smiled. He grabbed a stick and dramatically wound up as if at bat. *Bong!* Mr Corelli banged a large metal gong painted with a dollar symbol. Then he moved Tyler's name up the list hanging at the front of the class. Tyler pumped his fist excitedly.

Miley sighed. Things were not looking good.

Sarah stepped forward and placed her envelope in Mr Corelli's hand.

Mr Corelli's eyes lit up as he felt the weight of the envelope. "Sarah, show me the money!" He peeked inside the envelope and gasped. "Wow, dudette, how'd you raise so much?"

"Well, I learned good charity skills from my parents. They met at a Red Cross blood drive and then honeymooned in the Peace Corps, building aqueducts for – "

Bong! Mr Corelli smacked the gong, interrupting Sarah. "Great story," he said, fixing his bow tie. "Next!"

Miley, Lilly, and Oliver walked up to their teacher. Oliver tentatively handed over their skinny envelope.

"Ah, yes. The three amigos. Show me the money!" Mr Corelli peered inside their envelope. Then he looked closer, as if he had missed something. "Seriously," he said, frowning. "Show me the money."

"That's all we could raise," Miley admitted.

"Aren't you going to hit the gong?" Oliver asked.

"Oh, I've got a special one for you." Mr Corelli held up a small triangle. He tapped it gently, barely making a sound. The class laughed. Miley wanted to sink into the floor.

Lilly dragged her friends to the side of the classroom. She turned to Oliver and mimicked, "'Aren't you going to hit the gong?'"

Oliver shrugged. "It's better than no gong at all."

Miley tried to look on the bright side. "Okay, maybe we're not winning, but thanks to Sarah, neither are Amber and Ashley."

BONG!

The noise of the gong shook the classroom. Miley clapped her hands over her ears and turned around. Mr Corelli was dancing. Amber and Ashley stood next to him, grinning as if they'd just won a lifetime supply of lip gloss. Then Mr Corelli moved their names up the board – higher than Sarah's. "Last year's champions are at it again!" he cried, turning to admire the numbers on the board. "Looks like some-one's going for the two-peat."

Amber and Ashley strolled over to Miley, Lilly, and Oliver.

"How'd you get so much money?" Lilly demanded.

"Simple," Ashley said. "We just went to the B of D."

"What's that?" Oliver asked.

"The Bank of Dad," Amber replied with a smirk.

"That's so unfair," Lilly complained. "We worked so much harder than you."

"Yeah!" Miley agreed. "We walked ten miles, faked six accents, and sang 'The Twelve Days of Christmas' fifty-eight stinking times!"

"Wow, you're right," Amber said. "You did work harder."

"We're just smarter," Ashley added.

"And richer. *Ooooo!*" they squealed at the same time. They touched their index fingers together. "*Sssss!*"

Amber and Ashley patted Miley and Lilly on the back, then triumphantly returned to their seats. Miley took a deep breath and turned to her friends. "I don't care what it takes," she said. "This time, I refuse to let them get the better of us."

"Uh, Miley?" Oliver said.

"Not now, Oliver." Miley needed to think. Nothing was more important than figuring out how to beat Amber and Ashley.

Oliver shrugged, as if to say, "If that's the way you want it." He wondered how long it would take Miley and Lilly to discover the signs taped to their backs that said: "Still Dorky" and "Still Dorkier."

Chapter Three

Jackson stretched his legs as if warming up for a big race. He had to be quick on his feet today, and he didn't want to pull a muscle.

"This was a good idea, Coop," Jackson said to his friend once he was ready.

Cooper stood at the opposite end of a ping-pong table set up in the Stewart's yard.

"I told you, man," Cooper said, "with

ping-pong, you don't have to be tall, strong, or good looking."

"Exactly!" Jackson agreed. "Wait a minute. I'm good looking."

"Sure, you are," Cooper said, trying to sound convincing. "Now, grab a paddle and let's get our ping-pong on."

"Bring it on, baby!" Jackson said. He was pumped. He was going to practise with Cooper so that when he played his dad, he'd crush him.

Jackson missed the first ball Cooper served. And the second. And the third. Every time he swung, all he hit was air.

The fourth time, Jackson swung hard. He missed the ball again. And this time the paddle went flying out of his hand, across the table, and over Cooper's head. It crashed into the neighbour's bushes, and there was a screech.

"Sorry, Mr Fluffers!" Jackson called to the neighbour's cat.

Jackson and Cooper practised all afternoon. Game after game, Cooper pummelled Jackson with ping-pong ball after ping-pong ball. Jackson dove for cover with each serve. After a few hours, something finally clicked. Jackson was actually making contact with the ball, and it was going back and forth over the net. He was playing ping-pong!

A while later, a ball bounced over the net toward Jackson. He slammed the ball to the other side, winning the game.

"Yeah!" Jackson shouted. He had finally beaten Cooper! Jackson performed his victory dance, including his version of 'the worm'.

"Great," Cooper muttered as he watched

his friend slither on the ground. "Now I have to teach you to dance, too!"

❊ ❊ ❊

Miley ignored the pinging and ponging of the ball outside the kitchen window. She, Lilly, and Oliver had a plan, and they were about to put it into action. She peered out of the back door, watching for her father. Oliver and Lilly straightened a few stacks of coins on the kitchen table.

"Okay, here he comes!" Miley called. She rushed over to the table and sat beside her friends.

As Mr Stewart entered, the three kids sighed loudly.

"Wow, a three-part sigh. Usually when I hear a sigh like that, my wallet hurts," said Mr Stewart.

Miley used her sweetest look. "Daddy, I know you already gave a big donation, but

Amber and Ashley's parents – "

Mr Stewart cut her off. "Now, you know what I always say: you can buy a thirsty man a cow, and he'll have all the milk he wants, but it still won't be enough to wash down his cookies."

Satisfied that he'd made his point, Mr Stewart left the kitchen.

"What?" asked Lilly.

"Huh?" said Oliver, looking confused.

Miley had heard this lecture before, so she tried to explain it to her friends. "He said he's happy to give to charity, but this is a chance for us to learn to be creative and raise money ourselves." Miley wrinkled her nose. The last part was new. "And then something about cookies."

"Maybe Hannah can ask a few people," Lilly said.

Miley realized that she had a concert that night as her secret alter ego, Hannah Montana. "Maybe Hannah can ask *a lot* of people!" she cried.

❉   ❉   ❉

That night, the wild cheering of the crowd made Miley feel as if she were soaring. She loved being on stage as Hannah Montana. The rhythm of the music, the bright lights, the audience watching her every move — nothing could be better.

Hannah flipped her long, blonde hair, which was really a wig, and belted her song "Who Said" into the microphone. As she sang, she danced up and down the stage, wearing a denim skirt, cute jacket, and high-heeled black boots.

After she hit the final note of the song, Hannah spoke to her fans. "Thank you! Thank you all for coming tonight. Now,

before I start my next song, I would like to give a shout-out for a great charity called United People's Relief. So show your love and make a donation." Hannah waved her arms encouragingly.

The crowd sent up a huge cheer. Hannah smiled. Her plan to raise money was going to work! A hailstorm of coins flew at her. Money came from all directions. And it hurt!

Hannah raised her hands to protect her face. "Please, people! Paper money only. I bruise like a cantaloupe!"

Who knew charity work could be so dangerous?

Chapter Four

The next day when Miley went to sit down, the sofa was piled high with money. She pushed the stacks of bills aside and plopped down. Lilly and Oliver sat beside her, fanning themselves with some of the bills — five, tens, and even twenties!

"I can't believe how much Hannah pulled in last night," Oliver said. He had never seen so much money.

"I know!" Miley exclaimed. "And it was

easier than finding a mullet at a truckers' convention."

"Huh?" Lilly and Oliver said together.

Miley shook her head. "Y'all wouldn't last two minutes in Tennessee," she said.

"I just can't wait to see the look on Amber's and Ashley's faces when they find out we won," Lilly said.

Without missing a beat, Miley and Lilly launched into their best Amber and Ashley impersonations. "I can't believe we lost," they whined. *"Waaaah!"* They touched index fingers, and their *"Sssss"* sounded like air escaping from a balloon. Perfect!

The doorbell rang and Miley leaped up to open the front door. It was Sarah, holding a United People's Relief can.

Sarah, eyes downward, began the speech she had already repeated hundreds of times that day. "Hello, sir or madam, would you like to donate – " Sarah looked up and recognized her classmate. "Oh, hi, Miley. You live here?"

"Yeah, come on in, Sarah." Miley brought her into the living room. "So how's the collecting going?"

"Pretty good," Sarah replied. "I woke at four this morning so I could raise money at the fish market, and then I caught the end of the graveyard shift at the meat plant, then sunrise aerobics at The Yoga Mat, then – "

"You get up this early every morning?" Lilly asked, amazed.

"No, on Saturdays I sleep in till five-thirty," Sarah explained. "Then I go to an old folks' home to serve breakfast."

"Why am I not surprised?" Miley said quietly.

"I just really want that gift card so I can

buy a bunch of clothes and then donate them to needy children," Sarah said.

Oliver gulped. "Needy children?"

"You'd donate the *whole* gift card?" Miley asked, trying to process how unselfish Sarah was. "You wouldn't even buy yourself a pair of socks?"

Sarah gave a little laugh. "I already have two pairs of socks. A pair and a spare. Who needs more than that?"

"Normal people?" Lilly whispered to Oliver.

Miley felt guilty. If Sarah ever saw how many pairs of socks she had in her Hannah Montana closet . . .

"Whoa!" Sarah cried, noticing the piles of money on the sofa. "How did you guys raise so much money? You must have worked really, really hard."

Miley bit her lip and glanced at Lilly and

Oliver. How could they ever explain all that cash?

"Well, uh, actually – " Oliver started.

"We did this. . . uh. . .thing – " Lilly stammered.

Miley grabbed her two friends. "Excuse us," she said to Sarah. Then she dragged Lilly and Oliver into the kitchen.

"Guys, we've got to give her the Hannah money," Miley whispered.

"What?" cried Lilly.

"No," Oliver said.

"C'mon, she's worked harder than any of us," Miley insisted. "And she's the only one who did it for the right reasons."

"Reasons, *schmeasons*!" Lilly said. "I want a new skateboard!"

Miley gave her best friend a look. "Lilly, you know Sarah deserves to win. Besides," she said, perking up at the thought, "this way we'll still get to see Amber and Ashley crushed like the bugs they are!" Miley pretended to crush bugs with her shoe.

"Okay," Oliver agreed with a sigh. "Let's go give Miss Goody Two-socks the money."

They returned to Sarah, who was straightening the sign on her collection can.

"Hey, Sarah," Lilly said. "We decided. . . you should try the Brustroms down the street. They're loaded."

Miley flicked her friend on the arm.

"But," Lilly continued grudgingly, "in case they're not home, we want to make a donation to your fund-raising."

Miley scooped up an armful of money from the sofa, but Sarah gently pushed her away. "I can't take your money. You guys worked really hard."

"Not as hard as you," Oliver said earnestly.

"Trust us," Lilly said.

Sarah shook her head. "No. I couldn't sleep at night if I took credit for someone else's work. And that would be really bad considering how early I get up."

"It never ends," Miley said under her breath.

"Besides, I still have a chance to win. There's a carnival at the beach tonight. And if I stand under the Loopty-Loop, maybe I can catch some spare change." Then Sarah cringed. "While I dodge the vomit." She headed out the door. "Bye," she called.

"Y'all, we *have* to find a way to get her that money," Miley said.

"And maybe an umbrella," Oliver joked.

Lilly smiled. "I bet she'd take a donation from a generous celebrity."

Miley smiled, too. "I bet she would."

"Yeah, right. Where are we going to find

one of those?" Oliver asked.

Please tell me he's kidding, Miley thought. She and Lilly each grabbed a sofa cushion and hit Oliver on the head. Maybe that will knock some sense into him, Miley thought.

"Oh, right. Hannah," Oliver said, suddenly remembering. "You'd think I'd get it by now."

Chapter Five

Sweat dripped down Jackson's face. His lungs burned as he gasped for air.

Focus! Focus! he told himself. He knew victory was in sight if he just kept his eye on the ball.

"Wham!" he cried as he hit the ping-pong ball with his paddle. "Bam! Take that!" The ball cleared the net with the perfect amount of spin. "Slam!" he shouted as the ball zoomed past his father.

Jackson jumped up and down. "I did it, I won! Today, I am a man. I beat my daddy! I beat my daddy!" he sang with joy.

Mr Stewart was amazed. "Well, I'll be darned. You beat me. You actually beat me." After all these years Jackson had finally won, fair and square. Mr Stewart wasn't sure if he felt happy for his son or depressed for himself. He hoped this didn't mean he was getting old!

"Oh, come on, I didn't beat you. I *destroyed* you. I crushed you. I buried you under an avalanche of Jackson – "

Mr Stewart held up his hand. "Nobody likes a sore winner, son."

"Ooh, who's pouting now?" Jackson taunted.

"Nobody's pouting," Mr Stewart said, trying to look happy.

Jackson shrugged. "Whatever you say, Pouty McPoutpants."

His dad walked across the driveway toward a towel lying on the other side. "Okay, I'm just going to grab my towel and – "

Jackson darted from the opposite side of the ping-pong table. He sprinted toward the towel, and grabbed it first. "See that?" Jackson cried. "I beat you again."

"Come on, Jackson," his dad said. "It's not like I was trying to get to my towel first."

Jackson didn't care. He was on a winning streak – and it felt *good*. "Even if you were, you'd lose," he told his dad.

"You know, everything doesn't have to be a competition." Mr Stewart picked up a cold bottle of water.

Jackson quickly grabbed a bottle of

water, too. He locked eyes with his dad. Bring it on, his stare challenged.

Mr Stewart smiled. "Now you're just being silly."

"Am I?" Jackson raised an eyebrow.

At the same time, Jackson and his dad unscrewed the caps and chugged their waters.

Jackson gulped the water from his bottle and slammed it down first. Winner!

His dad stared in amazement.

"Ha!" Jackson yelled.

"Best two out of three?" Mr Stewart asked, reaching for another bottle.

"Oh, you are so on." Jackson was ready for the challenge.

Hours later, Jackson stared at all the empty water bottles piled on the living room coffee table. He wondered if maybe, just maybe, he wasn't quite up to this challenge. But it would have to snow in Malibu before Jackson would ever admit that to his dad.

"Still think you can hold it longer?" Mr Stewart asked. He was sitting next to Jackson on the sofa.

Jackson pulled his knees closer to his chest and rocked back and forth. The motion helped him not think about all the water inside him. All that water sloshing around, waiting to get out. "I could last all day. I'm like a camel. What about you?"

"I'm okay. Just maybe a little thirsty," said his dad, a mischievous glint in his eye.

Jackson picked up a pitcher of water from the table. "Well, let me help you out there," he said, grabbing a glass. Then very slowly he poured the water from the pitcher into the glass. He watched the stream of liquid flow. It was too much. If he waited much longer . . .

"Okay, you win!" Jackson yelled. He bolted from the sofa upstairs to the bathroom.

"I knew having eight brothers and sisters, and one outhouse would pay off someday," Mr Stewart said aloud to himself as he poured another glass of water.

Chapter Six

At the beach near Rico's Surf Shop, Miley was facing her own challenge. A carnival was set up on the sand, and the air smelled like candyfloss and popcorn. There was a Ferris wheel, bumper cars, a dunking booth, and lots of throw-a-softball-in-a-can—type games. But Miley and Lilly were on a mission. They didn't have time to play games. They ducked behind a large bin and watched Sarah, who was standing in front of a ball pit, holding her collection can. As parents walked their children toward the pit of small, colourful balls, Sarah held out her can.

"Thanks for contributing to United People's Relief," Sarah said as a man dropped a single coin into her can.

Miley nudged Lilly. It was time to help Sarah. Miley was dressed as Hannah in her long, blonde wig, and Lilly was wearing a short purple wig for her disguise as Lola Luftnagle, Hannah's best friend. Miley slipped on a pair of huge sunglasses and pulled her blue hoodie over her head. She hoped her disguise would work. Hannah always attracted *a lot* of attention – not what Miley wanted tonight. Also, there were several kids from school at the carnival. She didn't want anyone to discover that she was really a famous pop star.

"Let's just give her the money and get out of here before anyone spots Hannah," Lilly said. They hurried over to Sarah.

"Hey," Miley said.

"Hello, would you like to – " Sarah stopped in disbelief as Miley, disguised as Hannah, pulled down her hood and took off her glasses.

"Ha. . .you. . .Hann. . .her. . .'The Other Side'. . ."The Other Side". . .you. . ." Sarah tried to form the words, but she was too stunned that Hannah Montana was standing right in front of her. She fainted, hitting the ground with a soft thud.

"I'm guessing she's a fan," Lilly said.

"Ya think?" Miley said.

They both kneeled down and fanned their classmate.

"Sarah, come on, wake up. Sarah, look, there's a kitten up a tree," Miley said.

Always on the lookout to help others, especially baby animals, Sarah opened her eyes in response. "What? Kitten? For a minute I thought I saw – " Then she focused on Miley. "Hannah Montana!" she screamed, before fainting again.

A young girl overheard Sarah. "Look!" she cried. "It's Hannah Montana!"

Miley whipped her hood back on, just as the girl and her mother raced towards her. A crowd of people followed close behind.

"Oh, boy," Lilly said.

Miley grabbed Lilly's hand. "Quick, this way." They dashed across the carnival grounds. The crowd was at their heels. They weaved around the rides and game booths, hoping to lose all the Hannah fans.

They circled back to the ball pit. But the crowd wasn't far behind. Miley realized that there was nowhere else to run.

They were trapped!

Chapter Seven

Miley grabbed Lilly's hand and pulled her up the stairs to the top of the ball pit. They stood there, panting. They could hear the sound of running feet coming closer.

"Great plan," Lilly said, sarcastically. "Now what?"

There was only one choice. "Yippee ki-yea!" Miley yelled. She and Lilly jumped.

They landed in the pit and were quickly covered by hundreds of colourful balls.

Just then the crowd of fans reached the pit.

Moments later, Miley's and Lilly's heads popped up from the balls. Their wigs and jackets were gone. They looked like themselves instead of their alter egos.

"Where did she go? Where's Hannah Montana?" a girl called to them.

"There she goes," Miley and Lilly said together. But they pointed in different directions.

"I meant that way!" they cried, changing directions. Oh, no, Miley realized, they were still pointing in opposite directions.

She had an idea. "You better split up," Miley told the crowd. The fans were so eager to find Hannah that half of them ran one way and the other half ran the opposite direction.

"Quick," Lilly advised, "back to Sarah." They dived under the balls.

But when they came up, Miley had on Lola's wig and Lilly sported Hannah's blonde 'do. "Something ain't right," Miley said, looking at her friend.

"You look good in purple," Lilly said with a laugh.

"Thank you." Miley pulled Lilly back under with her. They wiggled in the darkness under the balls, trying to get dressed correctly. Miley felt as if there were six arms instead of four in there! She came up for air.

Now they were both zipped up in the same sweatshirt. "I know we're close, but this is ridiculous," Miley said.

Again they plunged into the colourful balls. This time they got it right. They climbed out of the ball pit looking like Hannah and Lola. Then they walked over to Sarah.

When she saw them, Sarah stood up, still in shock. "You, you – " she stammered.

"Want me to donate money to United People's Relief?" Miley, as Hannah again, interrupted. "I thought you'd never ask." Miley wanted to get this over with quickly, before Sarah passed out again or Hannah's fans tracked her down – or both. "Lola, give her the money."

Lilly held out an envelope stuffed with money to Sarah. But she was having trouble letting go of her dream of a new skateboard deck. Her fingers clenched the envelope tightly.

"Lola, release!" Miley commanded.

Lilly let go. Sarah peeked inside the envelope. "This is, wow, there must be. . . ohhh. . ." She looked as if she were about to faint again.

"You're welcome. Good-bye," Miley said

quickly. Time to wrap things up! She grabbed Lilly's hand, and they hurried away.

"So, that went well," Lilly said.

Miley nodded. "And thanks for pinching me back there in the ball pit."

"I didn't pinch you. You pinched *me*," Lilly said.

Suddenly they heard a giggle. An evil giggle.

They whirled around, just in time to see a little girl pop up from the ball pit. She smirked at them. Aha! There had been someone down there with them, Miley realized. Then she and Lilly turned toward home. She couldn't wait to see Sarah win the fund-raiser the next day.

Chapter Eight

Miley woke up the next morning feeling good. Today was the big day: the day that Amber and Ashley would lose, lose, lose!

At school, Miley watched Mr Corelli tally the donations at the front of the classroom. A reporter and photographer from the local newspaper stood in a corner, ready to interview the winner. Miley had to hold back her laughter as she watched

Amber and Ashley putting on lip gloss, convinced they'd get their pictures in the paper for winning.

"This is going to be so great," Miley told Lilly and Oliver.

"Yeah, after all our work, Sarah better be happy," Lilly said. She still wasn't quite over that skateboard deck.

"And she better buy herself a pair of socks," Oliver added. He still wasn't over the only-owning-two-pairs thing.

Mr Corelli rubbed his hands together in anticipation. "Okay, here's the moment you've all been waiting for. The winner of this year's fund-raiser is. . ." He paused and launched into an air-drumroll that seemed to go on forever.

"Mr Corelli," the class whined.

"Oh, right, sorry," he said, stopping his fake drumroll. ". . .Amber and Ashley!"

"Yea – *what*?!" Miley couldn't believe she had heard right. She stared at her teacher. Amber and Ashley squealed with joy.

Lilly stood up, outraged. "How could they have raised more money than Han–I mean us – I mean Sarah?"

Amber and Ashley strolled to the front of the room, as if walking the red carpet. They stopped in front of Miley and Lilly. "Once we found out that someone had raised more money than we did, we just asked our parents to write another check," Amber explained.

"Now, if you'll excuse us, we've got to do an interview for the newspaper," Ashley said. They hurried over to the reporter.

"I don't understand," Miley said. "How did they find out how much money we raised?"

Oliver slowly slid down in his seat.

"Oliver!" Lilly cried.

"Okay, maybe I bragged a *little* about how Sarah was going to beat them," he admitted.

"Button it," Miley said. She turned to Lilly. "I feel sorry for Sarah," Miley continued. "She's going to be crushed."

"Yay, good for you!" Sarah cheered loudly for Amber and Ashley. She stood up from her seat in the back of the room and clapped her hands.

"Yeah, she's taking it really hard," Lilly muttered.

Miley, Lilly, and Oliver walked over to Sarah. "Why are you so happy, Sarah?" Miley asked, confused. "I thought you wanted to win."

"It isn't about winning," Sarah explained. "It's about raising money for charity. And that's all that really matters."

Miley was impressed. "You know what, guys? She's right," she told her friends.

"A little annoying, but right," Oliver whispered to Lilly.

"It's just a shame that Amber and Ashley won," Lilly said. "They're never going to do all the good stuff Sarah would've done."

Suddenly, Miley had an idea. She grinned at her friends. "Who knows? They might surprise you." Miley walked to the front of the class, where Amber and Ashley were answering the reporter's questions. Her friends followed.

"We're just so happy for Universal Relief," Ashley said, flipping her ponytail.

"You mean United People's Relief," the reporter corrected.

Amber jumped in to help her friend. "Whatever you call it, people are going to be relieved."

Miley tapped the reporter's arm to get her attention. "And they didn't even tell you the best part," she said. Everyone looked at her, confused. Miley smiled. "They're going to use all the money from the gift card to buy clothes for needy children."

"Needy *who*?!" Amber and Ashley said together, their hands on their hips.

"Wow!" said the reporter, impressed. "You two are amazing. This is going to make a great story."

"Yeah, well, the truth is –" Ashley began.

Before she could worm her way out, Lilly cut her off. "But wait, there's more."

"No, there's not. Really," Ashley told the reporter. She was looking a little pale.

"Don't be so modest," Miley said. "Go ahead, Lilly."

Lilly smiled, enjoying herself. "They're going to spend their day off from school volunteering to wash dishes at the soup kitchen."

"Ewww!" Amber and Ashley exclaimed in disgust.

"I'll see you at the soup kitchen," Sarah said, happy to have found two more helpers.

"Be sure to wear your hairnets, girls," Miley said. She could already see the photo in the school trophy case this year: Amber and Ashley washing dishes and wearing dirty aprons, rubber gloves, and hairnets.

Miley looked at the gift card that she hadn't won. It didn't matter; everything had turned out great. She'd beaten Amber and Ashley at their own game – and helped needy children at the same time. Sometimes, Miley thought, it doesn't matter if you win or lose – it's that you tried your best, and your friends helped you do it.

PART TWO

Chapter One

It was a Saturday afternoon, and Miley's dad had called a family meeting. Miley wasn't worried. Her brother, Jackson, was always getting into trouble. Miley was eager to find out what he'd done this time.

Miley skipped from her bedroom down the stairs into the family room. She skidded to a stop when she saw Jackson. He sat curled in a chair, fidgeting nervously.

"Why did Dad call a family meeting?"

Jackson asked. "I hate family meetings."

"What'd you do?" Miley asked gleefully.

"What do you mean, what did I do? What did *you* do?" Jackson retorted.

"I didn't do anything." Miley grinned. "I *never* do anything."

"Look," Jackson said, "it doesn't matter who did what as long as we stay united, stay strong, and stand together – " He spotted their dad coming down the stairs. "She did it! She did it! I saw it with my own two eyes." He pointed to Miley. "You should be ashamed of yourself."

So much for unity. Miley scowled at her brother. "Way to stay strong, you gutless little weasel."

"Don't worry, Mile. I know you didn't do anything," her dad said.

Miley grinned at Jackson triumphantly.

Mr Stewart turned toward his son and

gave him a long, intense stare.

Uh-oh, Miley thought, Jackson's a goner.

"I didn't do anything either," her brother protested.

"I know," Mr Stewart said, still staring.

"Then why are you looking at me like that?" Jackson asked fearfully.

"It's fun," Mr Stewart said with a laugh.

"You are a cruel, cruel father." Jackson shook his head at his father's sense of humour.

"Oh, yeah? Would a 'cruel, cruel father' give you these?" Mr Stewart held up two shiny new credit cards.

Jackson gave his dad a bear hug.

Miley was stunned. Her dad handed her the credit card, and she stared at it. *Her* credit card! She had never seen a more beautiful piece of plastic in her life.

"My very first credit card," she said in a breathy voice. Choir music filled her head. A bright light illuminated the card. It was a magical moment. "Today, I am a woman!" she cried.

"And I'm still a dad," Mr Stewart said. "And these cards are for emergencies only."

The music in Miley's head stopped. The bright lights went dark. Miley snapped back to reality. What?

Jackson stepped back from his dad. "You could've told me that before I wasted the hug."

"Look, the point is, these are just in case you get into trouble and I'm not around," Mr Stewart explained, handing them the cards. Then he crossed his arms and stared at his son.

"Why are you staring at me again?" Jackson asked nervously.

Part One

Miley couldn't wait for school to be over.
She and Lilly were planning to do some
serious shopping.

"May the best fund-raiser win," Ashley said.

Lilly and Miley couldn't figure out why their classmates kept whispering and laughing.

"This is as close as you'll ever get to one of these," Ashley said.

"One, two, three, let's bring the cha-ching!"
the three friends shouted together.

Oliver, Miley, and Lilly launched into
"The Twelve Days of Christmas."

"Wow, a three-part sigh. Usually when I hear
a sigh like that, my wallet hurts,"
said Mr. Stewart.

"I'd like to give a shout-out for a great charity called
United People's Relief," Miley said
as Hannah.

Part Two

"Where do you think I should put my credit card?"
Miley asked Jackson.

"I promised my dad I'd use this for emergencies
only," Miley said.

"It's free food. I'm a guy. Do the math,"
Oliver said.

"How much for these shoes?" Miley asked.

"Why do I feel a sudden breeze?" asked Miley.

Miley held up a cute white skirt with ruffles.

"Say hello to the carousel of cash," Jackson said.

"I kind of sold them to you by mistake, and I'd really like to buy them back," Miley, as Hannah, explained.

Mr Stewart shrugged. "It's still fun."

"Thank you so much, Daddy. I promise, you won't regret this," Miley said. "'Cause we're both mature enough to handle this responsibility." She gave her brother a don't-you-dare-mess-this-up look. "Right, Jackson?"

"Absolutely." Then Jackson's smile faded. He patted his jeans pockets furiously. "Okay, I lost my card. Wait, you handed it to me, right?"

"And I've regretted it ever since." Mr Stewart shook his head in amazement.

Jackson dropped to his hands and knees. He frantically searched the floor under the coffee table. Miley heard him let out a huge sigh of relief.

"Oh, there it is." Jackson held up the credit card. "And my toothbrush!" He waved a blue toothbrush in the air. "I've been looking for this since Tuesday."

Gross! Miley thought. "You haven't brushed since Tuesday?"

"Miles, don't be stupid," said Jackson as he stood up. "I've been using yours."

"Ewww!"

After rushing to her bathroom to replace her toothbrush, Miley spent the next several hours admiring her new credit card. It looked good with all kinds of outfits – the perfect fashion accessory.

She sat on a stool at the kitchen counter, slipping the card in and out of her wallet. "Where do you think I should put my credit card?" she asked.

Jackson was busy piling meats, cheese, and tomato slices on bread. Sandwich-making was a sport to him.

"Should I put it in the little window where everybody can see it? Or is that too showy?" Miley moved the card from place to place. "Yeah, maybe I should just put it in one of the slots. That says I have a credit card, but I ain't bragging about it." She turned the wallet to show Jackson.

"I don't care," he said. "Guys don't worry about dumb stuff like that. Just give me a card and a pocket to put it in." He patted the back pocket of his jeans. He patted it again. Then he patted his other pockets. His eyes opened wide. "Where did I put that thing?"

"Don't worry, it's probably right next to your brain," Miley said. Then she bit her nails, pretending to be horrified. "Uh-oh, now you'll *never* find it."

She watched Jackson hurry to the family room to search for his card. She shook her head. Trusting Jackson with a credit card was like asking him to pick up Hannah's dry cleaning: really not a good idea.

Just then, Lilly and Oliver rolled through the open front door on their skateboards. "Where is it?" Lilly shouted.

"Let me see it!" Oliver added.

"Where is it?" Lilly repeated.

Miley held up her wallet. "There it is, third slot from the top," she said proudly. Her two best friends gasped in awe.

"Nice placement," Oliver said.

"Thank you." Miley joined them in admiring her credit card.

"Can I hold it?" Lilly asked reverently.

"Sure. But edges only," Miley warned.

"Duh." Lilly knew the unwritten rules of credit-card behaviour.

Miley slipped her card out of its slot and passed it to Lilly.

"It's beautiful!" Lilly gushed.

But instead of admiring the card, Oliver looked directly over Miley's shoulder – toward the untouched sandwich Jackson had left on the counter. "I think I'm in love," Oliver said, walking into the kitchen. "You're wearing avocado, aren't you?" he asked the sandwich as he reached for it. "You know what that does to me." He growled and took a huge bite.

"What is *wrong* with you, boy?" Miley demanded.

Oliver took another bite. "It's free food. I'm a guy. Do the maths."

"Where is that card?!" Jackson cried from the family room. He searched under each sofa cushion.

"Ow!" Oliver crunched down on something hard. He pulled the sandwich away and took a plastic card from his mouth. "I think I found it."

Jackson smacked himself on the fore-head. "That's right. I used it to spread the mustard."

Miley and Lilly rolled their eyes. Oliver shrugged, put the card on the counter, and kept on eating.

Lilly nudged Miley. "Hello, what are we standing around here for? There's a huge flea market at the beach today." Lilly held Miley's credit card up to her ear. "And what's that, cardy?" she asked, pretending the card was whispering to her. "I wanna go, I wanna go, I wanna go. Let me go, please, please, please," Lilly said in a high-pitched voice, pretending to be the credit card.

Miley took back her card. "Lilly, I prom-ised my dad I'd use this for emergencies only. Now, of course, I'll go to the flea mar-ket with you, but only to look – I'm defi-nitely not buying anything."

Chapter Two

A little while later, Miley felt as if she was in paradise.

The area outside Rico's, their favourite beachside hangout, had been taken over by a huge flea market. Table after table was piled high with clothes, handbags, hand-made jewellery, and hair accessories. Some booths were selling electronics, skateboards, and surfboards. Miley knew shopping, and she could tell that this was a good flea market.

She pulled Lilly and Oliver to a nearby booth. She held up a pair of leather sandals from the table. The leather was so soft. "I have to have these shoes," Miley said.

"Why?" Oliver asked.

Miley rolled her eyes. "They're shoes. I'm a girl. Do the maths." She turned to the guy manning the booth. He was tall with dark hair and jet black eyes. "Excuse me, sir, how much for these shoes?"

"For you, today, seventy-five," the man said with a heavy accent.

"Seventy-five cents?!" Miley squealed. Score! Was she a good shopper or what? "She'll take a pair, too," Miley said, pointing toward Lilly. "And a matching belt."

The man laughed. "Oh, pretty and *funny*. Seventy-five dollars, and don't pretend to be surprised, rich Malibu child." The man sneered at her.

"Wow, I don't have that," Miley said, blushing.

The salesman reached over and lifted the sandals out of her hands. "Wow, then you don't have shoes."

Miley reached for the sandals. They were so pretty! But the salesman held on to them firmly.

Oliver pulled his friends aside. "Miley, it's a flea market. They want you to bargain," he whispered.

"I know, but I'm no good at it," Miley whispered back.

"Well, lucky for you, I am. Just follow my lead." Oliver headed back to the booth.

"Look," he said to the salesman, "I know you said you wanted seventy-five for these shoes, but we both know you'll take twenty-five. So I'll make it easy for you. She'll give you thirty."

Miley grabbed Oliver's arm and whispered in his ear. "I only have twenty-five."

Oliver turned back to the salesman. "You hesitated. I'm dropping to twenty-five."

"You drive a hard bargain," the man said. "Tell you what. For you, eighty-five."

"But it was just seventy-five," Oliver protested.

"That was before you made me mad," the man explained.

"Yeah? Well, now you've made *me* mad," Oliver retorted. "And you've just lost a sale."

"I don't care," the man said.

"Well, we're going to take our money and go," Oliver replied.

"Okeydokey." The salesman shrugged and began to fix his display.

"That's it, we're going," Oliver said loudly. He turned and walked away.

"Bye-bye," the salesman said.

Miley gazed longingly at the sandals, then hurried after Oliver. "But I want my shoes," she protested.

"Trust me," Oliver said, "he's just about to cave."

"Young lady, wait!" the salesman called.

"Ha!" Oliver looked victorious. "Told ya."

Miley, Lilly, and Oliver turned back expectantly.

"You have a doggy no-no on your shoe." The salesman pointed to Miley's white trainer.

Miley lifted her trainer off the sand. *Ewww!* Her face fell.

"Aw, man." Miley sat on a nearby wood plank to inspect the damage. "I wanted new shoes, not 'doggy no-no' shoes. This stinks."

Lilly held her nose. "Tell me about it."

It's time to get out of here, Miley thought. She stood – and heard a loud *rüipppp*! Her eyes widened. Uh-oh. "Why do I feel a sudden breeze?" she asked.

Lilly quickly looked behind Miley. "Because your back door's open."

Miley gasped and looked around. It was only a matter of time before she saw someone from school. "Quick, Lilly, hide me!" Miley quickly hid behind her friend.

"Over there," Lilly instructed, pointing to a booth. "They sell skirts." They walked across the sand as one – Lilly never more than an inch away.

Oliver suddenly veered off course, turning to the right. "Awesome skateboards." He started toward a different booth.

"Where?" Lilly turned to follow Oliver and left Miley behind.

Miley panicked and grabbed her friend. "It can wait!"

Together, the two friends shuffled over to the booth selling skirts.

"Excuse me," Miley called to the man inside the booth.

The salesman turned around, and the three friends gasped. It was the same guy from the shoe booth! Miley thought.

"May I help you?" the salesman asked.

"Weren't you just over there?" Miley demanded, pointing down the beach.

"No, that is my brother. Tough cookie, huh?" he replied.

"I'll say. He wanted me to give him seventy-five dollars for a pair of shoes." Miley was still outraged.

"Oh, he's terrible," the salesman agreed. "I'll give you a much better price."

Miley perked up. She held up a cute

white skirt with ruffles. "Great, how much for this skirt?"

"Seventy-four-ninety-five."

What's with these prices? Miley thought. "I can't afford that," she admitted.

"Twenty-five or we walk!" Oliver piped in on Miley's behalf.

Miley'd had enough of Oliver's bargaining. Her pants were split open and she needed something to wear – immediately. "*You* walk! I'm gettin' a sunburn where I shouldn't!"

Lilly placed her hand on Miley's arm to calm her down. "Miley, think about it. This is a real emergency. You could use your emergency credit card!"

That was a great idea. Then Miley heard her dad's voice in her head, talking about responsibility. "I don't know, Lilly – "

"I see London, I see France, I see someone's underpants!" cried a little girl behind Miley. People all over the beach turned to stare. The girl giggled uncontrollably, until her mother dragged her away.

No more thinking was needed. This was officially an emergency, Miley decided. She pulled her credit card out from her wallet and handed it to the salesman. "Okay, fine. Charge it."

The man smiled. "Just for you, I'll throw in this lovely belt – "

Miley breathed a sigh of relief. Everything was going to be okay now. "Oh, thank you."

"For twenty dollars more," the salesman added gleefully.

"Hey, you do need something to hold up the skirt," Lilly pointed out.

"Very true," Miley agreed. Besides, the thick, brown leather belt was awesome.

"And you know what would look great with the skirt and the belt?" Lilly said, eyeing a pair of leather sandals that looked just like the ones at the other booth.

The salesman held them up. "These shoes?"

Miley looked at the sandals. The ones that suddenly matched the new skirt and belt. The ones that now made a lot of sense. She smiled. It was time to let her new credit card work its emergency magic.

Chapter Three

Miley tried to balance three shopping bags and a small, rolled-up rug in her arms. It was a good thing that her new outfit — skirt, belt, sandals, tank top, jacket, sunglasses, and hat — was so comfortable. Shopping was a megaworkout. Her arm muscles ached under the weight of all her purchases.

"Hey, Jackson," she called, as she walked into the family room.

Her brother was bent over the large planters next to the piano.

"Okay, I did not lose my credit card again. It's exactly where I put it, or left it, or dropped it." He lifted a planter and looked underneath. "Oh, Dad's going to have a cow," he moaned. He turned toward Miley. Suddenly his expression changed from worry to delight. "Of course," he said, moving closer to check out all Miley's shopping bags, "when he sees what *you've* done, he's going to have the whole barn."

"It's an emergency," Miley insisted.

"Where do you want these, Miley?" Lilly called. She stumbled through the door under the weight of eight more shopping bags.

"A really *big* emergency," Miley added.

"Oh, my fingers are cramping," Oliver complained, as he staggered through the door. The boxes in his arms were piled so high that Miley could barely see his face. "Hey, can I use that electric hand-massager you bought?" he asked.

Jackson bounced up and down gleefully. This was too good! "Hand-massager?" he asked his sister. "Expensive electric hand-massager?"

Miley put down her bags and rolled her eyes. Jackson could be so clueless. "Okay, all right? Imagine this. I'm up on stage, ya know, holding that microphone . . ." Miley pretended she was Hannah with a microphone in her hand. ". . . with all that singing, and I'm dancing when all of a sudden, my hand cramps up." Miley faked a look of pain. "I have to stop the whole concert and disappoint thousands of people. Or, hand-massager."

Miley smiled at Jackson. Suddenly the smile froze on her face as she realized how ridiculous she sounded.

"Okay, fine. It made sense when I was signing for it," she admitted.

"How did the carpet make sense?" Jackson asked curiously.

"The guy said it would match my shoes," Miley said with a groan. "Oh, man, I blew it big-time!"

"Yes, you did," Jackson agreed happily. "Ooh, I can't wait for the next family meeting when Dad gives you The Look." Jackson mimicked their dad and stared at Miley.

She was toast, Miley thought. She sighed and sat down on the piano bench, accidentally pressing on the keys. All of a sudden, a credit card popped up from the open piano top.

"There you are!" Jackson caught the card in midair. "You joker, you are such a card. Yes, you are." He held up his credit card for Miley to see. "A clean, pure, unswiped beauty. Unlike somebody's dirty, soiled, little maxed-out mess."

"Okay. Whatever can be maxed out can be maxed back in." Miley was not a girl who gave up. "The guy gave me a one-hundred-per cent money-back guarantee. So all we have to do is take this stuff back to the flea market."

Lilly and Oliver gazed at all the bags and boxes and groaned.

Miley piled all her purchases back into her friends' arms and grabbed her share. There was no time to waste. She was on a mission. She had to get back to the beach – fast!

A few minutes later, Miley and her friends reached the beach. They stared in shock. The beach was completely empty. No booths, salesmen, or flea market. Only sand, sun, and ocean.

"What happened? Where'd everybody go? Where's the guy?" Miley cried.

"And his brother?" Oliver asked.

"Boy, when they say one day only, they're not kidding," Lilly said, amazed.

"Oh, man, I can't believe this." Miley shook her head. "Now there's only one thing left to do."

"Come clean and tell your dad?" Oliver asked.

"Heck no, that's crazy talk." Miley rolled her eyes. "No, I'm talking about the other 'only one thing.'"

"You wouldn't!" Oliver said, realizing her plan.

"You can't!" Lilly warned.

"I have to!" Miley decided she had no choice. In order to get out of this kind of trouble, she needed the most scheming, twisted mind of all. She needed the help of . . . her brother.

Chapter Four

Miley and Jackson stood inside a secret room in the Stewart house. It was Miley's favourite place of all – Hannah Montana's closet.

An enormous carousel of designer clothes took up most of the carpeted room. The rack moved electronically. With the touch of a button, Miley could check out all the outfits that she wore as Hannah Montana to her concerts, to movie premieres, and magazine and video shoots. Display cases of sparkly jewellery, cool sunglasses, and cute handbags were lined up along one side of the room. Hundreds of shoes were stacked by colour and heel size along another wall.

"Mile, it's simple," Jackson explained. "All you have to do is pay off that credit-card bill before Dad ever sees it. And to do that, you need money." He flicked a switch and the rack of clothes slowly swung around. "Say hello to the carousel of cash."

"I can't sell Hannah Montana stuff," Miley protested. "I use it."

"Miles, you auction off some of this stuff on the internet and your problems are solved," Jackson explained. "There are clothes here you've outgrown and things you never even wear." He walked over to a display case and picked up a velvet box.

Inside was a pair of glittering faux diamond-and-blue-sapphire earrings. "What about these earrings?"

"Those are important." Miley held up the earrings. "I used them in a video shoot last month. . ." And then it hit her. ". . .and I'll probably never wear them again." Maybe her brother was on to something.

"Exactly. But some lucky girl out there will, and she'll pay through the nose for the chance." Jackson opened the laptop that he'd brought along and pulled up a page that said: *Exclusive Hannah Montana Memorabilia*. Jackson had created a website to sell Hannah's stuff! "Oh, that reminds me," he said. He pulled a tissue from a box on a nearby table. "A used Hannah Montana tissue will go for $37.95."

"How do you know that?" Miley asked her brother.

"That sinus infection you had last year helped pay for my car," he explained. He held the tissue up to her nose. "Now, blow – Daddy needs a new set of spinners."

Disgusting! Miley thought. Then she remembered that her massive credit-card bill would arrive any day now. She sneezed into the tissue as hard as she could. These were desperate times!

For the next several days, Miley and Jackson spent every free moment sorting through Hannah's outfits. Miley boxed and wrapped it all – including the video-shoot earrings. Jackson handled the website auctions and secretly mailed the packages from the post office. Luckily, their dad hadn't caught on – yet.

When Miley was sure that she had nothing else left to sell, Jackson began punching the numbers into an adding machine. "And the grand total is. . ." he announced dramatically as he hit the TOTAL button.

Miley and Jackson stared at the number. "Wow!" they said together.

Miley squealed with happiness. "I never thought I'd say this: Jackson, I love you." She hugged her brother.

Jackson wriggled away. "Love, *schmuv*. I'm still getting my forty per cent."

"Ten," Miley said.

"Thirty," Jackson negotiated.

"Ten," Miley repeated.

"Twenty," Jackson tried.

"Ten," Miley insisted.

Jackson gave in. "Fine."

There was a knock at the door. "Hey, Mile, you in there?" Mr Stewart called.

Miley's eyes opened wide. "Quick, hide the stash. It's the Man!" She pushed the cash and the adding machine toward Jackson.

Jackson looked around for a place to hide. His choices were limited. He scurried up three carpeted stairs and dove under the clothes carousel.

"Come in." Miley tried to make her voice sound normal. She dropped into a big, purple, cushioned chair and leaned back, as if she'd been chilling there for hours.

Her dad walked into the dressing room and gave her a questioning look.

"Hi, Daddy. I was just. . ." Miley reached down and grabbed a handbag that was on the floor. ". . .reading my purse." She pulled out a little white piece of paper from inside the purse and read it. "This one was inspected by Inspector Fifteen. I love her work."

"Sorry to bother you, honey." Luckily,

her dad hadn't noticed the guilty look on her face – or Jackson hiding underneath the carousel clothing rack. "I just need those earrings back that you used in that video shoot last month."

Miley couldn't believe it. "What earrings? What video? What month?" she babbled.

"You know, the fake blue-sapphire-and-diamond ones that they let us keep? Well, it turns out they gave us the real ones instead. They want them back." Mr Stewart laughed. "Do you believe that?"

This is so *not* funny, Miley thought. She played along and laughed with her dad. "No. Hey, here's a funny thought: how about we just buy them?"

Her dad laughed harder. "Sure, if you have a quarter of a million dollars burnin' a hole in your britches."

"*What?!*" Miley exclaimed.

There was a loud *bang!* from the carousel. The rack spun around, revealing Jackson, who had practically fainted at the news.

"Jackson, what are you doing in there?" Mr Stewart asked.

Jackson raised his head. "Oh, I, uh, like to nap here sometimes. The motion is soothing."

"Normally, I'd pursue that," Mr Stewart said, giving his son a puzzled look. "But right now, I'm concerned; I'm on the hook for a quarter of a million dollars."

Miley started to sweat. They were in *huge* trouble now. "You hear that, Jackson?" she said through gritted teeth. "*A quarter of a million dollars.*"

Jackson looked wildly between his dad and his sister. "It seems like you two have a lot to talk about. I'll just take another spin around the park." He reached out, slammed the ON button for the clothes carousel, and disappeared behind the wall.

"So, where are the earrings?" Mr Stewart asked as he walked toward the jewellery display case.

Miley grabbed her dad's arm to stop him. "Right, the earrings. Yes. The earrings. They are. . .They're at. . ." She tried to think up a good explanation. Anything.

"At Lilly's?" her dad offered.

"Okay," Miley agreed. "I'll get 'em back to you as soon as I can." She led her dad toward the door. "But right now I. . .I. . . I need to be alone with my clothes."

"Are you okay?" he asked suspiciously.

"Of course. I'm fine. I'm a girl; we do that," Miley replied. She pretended to be mellow and calm. "Shoo, shoo. Out, out,

out." She gently pushed her dad out the door.

Mr Stewart glanced back. "What about your brother?"

"Let sleeping brothers lie," Miley said, closing the door after her dad. She spun around. Jackson now stood in front of her holding an envelope.

"This is all your fault." She pointed an accusing finger at him. "If I go down, you're goin' down with me, bub."

Jackson raised the envelope so Miley could read the return address. "Nobody's going anywhere except to 400 Grand Street. The home of Katherine McCord – otherwise known as the girl who bought your earrings."

"You really think she'd give them back?" Miley asked.

"Not to you," Jackson said. "But maybe to Hannah Montana."

Chapter Five

Later that day, Miley stepped out of Jackson's car dressed as Hannah Montana. She squinted at the address on the building. Yep, this was it: 400 Grand Street. Then she looked at the sign by the front door: RETIREMENT VILLA. Something wasn't right.

She pushed open the glass double doors and walked into a large rec room. She looked around and saw that the room was filled with senior citizens. Some were playing cards, some were watching TV, and others were sleeping.

"Are you sure this is the right address?" Miley asked Jackson, who was dressed as Hannah's chauffeur. She pointed around the room. "I mean, it looks like it's been a while since anyone here has 'pumped up the party.'"

Jackson seemed to be confused, too. "It's the right address. Maybe you have a bunch of older fans you never even knew about. Here, let me try something." He stepped into the middle of the room. "Hey, it's Hannah Montana!" he shouted.

Silence. Miley looked around. Usually if Hannah's name was yelled out in a public place, she was mobbed by fans in seconds. Here, nothing.

Jackson shrugged. "Okay, maybe not."

"My daughter lives in Montana." An elderly lady playing cards at a nearby table reached out and grabbed Jackson's hand.

"How nice for you," Jackson said, pulling away.

Miley scanned the room. "She's got to be around here somewhere." She leaned toward the lady playing cards with an elderly man. In her sweetest voice, she asked: "Oh, excuse me, do you know a Katherine McCord?"

The woman smiled. "Oh, yes. Yes, I do." She turned her attention back to the cards in her hand.

"Is she here?" Miley asked.

"Yes, she is." The woman pulled an ace from the deck and stared at it.

Miley waited. The woman slowly placed the ace with her other cards. At this rate, it'll be next Tuesday before we finish this conversation, Miley realized. "Where is she?" Miley prompted.

The man across the table spoke up. "That's her in the wheelchair." He pointed across the room to a woman asleep in a wheelchair.

Miley and Jackson walked over to her. She didn't look like the typical Hannah Montana fan.

"She's Katherine McCord?" Miley asked, puzzled. "She bought my earrings?"

"And she's wearing them." Jackson pointed to the expensive earrings hanging from the woman's ears. They looked really fancy compared with her knitted hat, long skirt, ruffled blouse, and button-down jumper. Jackson leaned toward the woman. "Ma'am? Ma'am?"

Ms McCord kept sleeping, however.

"Wow, I haven't seen somebody this out

since Uncle Earl thought he could last three minutes in the ring with that boxing kangaroo," Miley joked.

Jackson slowly crept closer to Ms McCord until he stood only inches away.

"What are you doing?" Miley whispered.

"I'm just going to take the earrings off gently and leave the money on her lap." Jackson reached toward her ear. His fingers brushed the earrings – and Ms McCord's eyes opened.

"*Aahhh!*" Jackson cried, as he stumbled backward.

The old woman smiled. "You want to get that close, you've got to buy me dinner, sailor."

"Excuse me, ma'am," Miley apologized.

Ms McCord looked at her and beamed. "Hey, you're Hannah Montana. Thanks for the earrings."

"Yeah, about that. See, I kind of sold them to you by mistake, and I'd really like to buy them back," Miley explained.

"Ooh, and I'd like to be president of these forty-eight states, but that isn't going to happen either," Ms McCord retorted. She began to roll her chair away.

"But –" Miley began.

Jackson grabbed the handles on the wheelchair and spun Ms McCord back around. He put on his best game-show-host voice. "But wait," he said, pretending that she'd won the grand prize. "If you act right now, we'll throw in two VIP concert tickets with backstage passes and preferred. . .wheelchair parking."

Miley turned the chair so Ms McCord was facing her. "All this can be yours," she said, playing along, "if you let me buy back my earrings, which are, of course, completely worthless."

Ms McCord shook her head. "Not to me. You see, I bought these because I thought they'd make me look younger."

"Unless she's a hundred and eight, it's not working," Jackson muttered quietly.

But not quietly enough. Ms McCord had heard the comment. "I'll have you know, ever since I put these on, Burt over there can't take his eyes off me." She waved at an elderly man sitting on the piano bench. He blew a kiss at her.

Miley decided to try a different approach. "You don't understand," she told Ms McCord. "These earrings are worth – "

" – the world to her, because they belonged to her grandmother," Jackson finished.

What was her brother talking about?

Miley wondered. Then she got it. "Yes, yes, they did," she said, playing along. "In fact, she wore them on her wedding day."

"Oh. Well, now that's different," said Ms McCord. "Of course I'll return them."

"Oh, thank you so much." Miley reached over to hug the woman.

Ms McCord stopped her. "But only to your grandmother," she explained. "I can't trust you, blondie. You sold them in the first place."

"But. . ." Miley objected.

"Is that a problem?" Ms McCord asked.

Miley pulled herself together. "No. Of course not. Actually Grandma's down the hall visiting a friend right now," Miley improvised.

Jackson didn't miss a beat. "That's right. She is."

"Well, go get her — and make it fast,"

Ms McCord commanded. "I've got water aerobics in ten minutes, and I want to get a good noodle."

Miley wasn't sure exactly how important it was for Ms McCord to nab a decent water floatie, but she decided they'd better hurry up. Miley grabbed Jackson and rushed down the hall. How was she going to convince someone who lived here to pretend to be her grandmother?

Chapter Six

Miley pushed a wheelchair into the main room. She plastered a smile on her face and glanced at her new grandma – Jackson in disguise. As "Grandma," he wore a lavender cardigan jumper, a long skirt, white lace gloves, glasses, and bright red lipstick. Miley just hoped that the curly grey wig he was wearing stayed on long enough for them to get the earrings back.

"Miss McCord," Miley said, stopping in

front of her. "I'd like to introduce you to my nana. . ." Miley tried to think of a good name. ". . .Nana Montana."

"Well, aren't you a cute young thing," Jackson said in an old lady's voice.

Ms McCord smiled. "It's been a while since anybody's called me that."

Nana Montana raised her hand to her ear. "I hear that. Barely."

The two old women laughed together at the joke. Miley breathed a sigh of relief. So far, so good.

"So, Nana, don't you want those earrings back that mean more to you than life itself?" Miley prompted.

"Why, yes. Yes, I do," Nana Montana said.

"Oh, I'm sorry for the misunderstanding." Katherine reached to take off the earrings. "Let me give these back to you."

Then she stopped and folded her hands in her lap. "But first, I could really use a glass of water."

"Of course," Jackson said. "Hannah will get that for you. Won't you, dear?"

"Sure," Miley said.

"And one for me," Nana Montana called. "Lemon wedge. No ice."

Miley forced a smile and headed toward the kitchen. "Of course."

Ms McCord leaned closer to Nana Montana. "So, you wore these earrings on your wedding day? I want to hear all about it."

Jackson had no idea how long it would take Miley to get back. He would have to wing it. "Oh, yes, of course. Morris was in the service. He invented the *Morris* code, you know. I'll never forget his proposal. Dot, dot, dash, dot, dash, dot."

"Oh, how romantic," Ms McCord said.

"I know; it still gives me the chills," Nana Montana confided.

Just then, the woman from the card table shuffled by.

"It's the air-conditioning," the woman piped up. "It's like living in a meat locker."

To fill the time until Miley returned, Jackson continued his story. He was still talking when his sister returned. "It was a beautiful wedding. I'll never forget dancing with President Lincoln," he said as Nana.

Ms McCord laughed. Miley gaped at her brother. President *Lincoln*? That would make Nana Montana over 150 years old! Jackson had never been very good at history, Miley thought.

"Nana, you and your stories," she teased, then changed the subject. "So what about those earrings?"

"Don't rush us, honey, we're having a nice talk." Ms McCord waved her closer. "Now make yourself useful and rub my neck."

Miley looked at the earrings still firmly attached to Ms McCord's ears. She had no choice. Miley, still dressed as Hannah Montana, rubbed the woman's neck.

"Save some TLC for me," Jackson said with a grin.

Miley shot him the evil eye. "Oh, I'm saving a little something for you all right, 'Nana.'"

The chores for Hannah didn't end there. She had to brush Ms McCord's hair – and Jackson's, too.

Then she had to give Ms McCord and Jackson manicures. Miley glared at her brother as the two "old ladies" chatted away.

Then she had to rub Ms McCord's feet. But there was absolutely no way she was touching her brother's stinky toes!

Next, Miley went to run the water for bubble baths.

The entire time Jackson was telling stories. ". . .and then Kong put me down to fight the airplanes – "

Miley'd had enough. She shoved the fluffy bath towels and shower caps at Ms McCord and Nana. "Okay guys, I got your bathtubs filled, but I'm not helping either of you into it. Now, *please*, how about those earrings?"

"Oh, the earrings. Yeah, I almost forgot," Ms McCord said. She removed them and held them out.

Miley reached for the sparkly earrings, but Ms McCord pulled them out of reach. "But first, I feel like a slice of rhubarb pie – "

"Okay, that's it, Grandma!" Miley said angrily. She had been pushed too far. "Give me back those earrings!"

Ms McCord held the earrings tightly in her fist. Miley tried to take them, but the woman wouldn't let go.

"Not without my pie!" she cried.

Miley pulled Ms McCord's hand open, and the earrings flew through the air.

Miley dived for the earrings as they fell to the floor. Before she could reach them, however, an old man wearing a big floppy hat rolled his wheelchair over and scooped up the earrings.

"Hey, those are my earrings! What are you doing?" Miley cried.

The man turned around and took off his hat. Miley's heart almost stopped. It was her dad!

"I'm trying to teach my kids a lesson

about keeping things from their father," he explained. He walked over to Nana Montana and plucked the wig off her head. Jackson smiled meekly.

Ms McCord laughed and gave Mr Stewart a high five. "Ha-ha, we got you!"

Stunned, Miley stared at them.

"Thanks for helping me out, Katherine," her dad said.

"My pleasure. I haven't had this much fun since I performed on Broadway. . ." Ms McCord tapped Jackson on the chin. ". . .for President Lincoln, you sweet little twit."

Jackson shrugged. "Cut me some slack. That wig was pretty tight."

"I'm sorry, Daddy," Miley said. "I should've come to you as soon as I messed up. But I just didn't want you to think of me as irresponsible."

"Well, I hope that you learned that the longer you avoid coming clean, the dirtier things get," Mr Stewart said. "Which reminds me. You're going to be cleaning out the garage and several other places until you get that credit card paid off."

"But, Daddy, there's spiders in the garage," Miley complained.

Her dad gave her The Look.

"I'll wear gloves," Miley decided.

"Hey, how'd you find out?" asked her brother.

"I've had my eye on those Internet auctions ever since I saw *someone* was selling used Hannah nose-blowers," Mr Stewart said.

Jackson slowly began to roll his wheelchair away. "I just want to point out that's a victimless crime."

"Oh, there's going to be a victim, all right," Mr Stewart warned.

Jackson quickly rolled across the room and out the back door.

"Daddy, aren't you going to go after him?" Miley asked.

"He won't get far," Mr Stewart replied.

"Yeah, I guess he's got to stop at the pool," Miley agreed.

"*Whooooaaa!*" Jackson's scream echoed throughout the retirement villa, followed by a loud *splash!*

Mr Stewart smiled. "We'll take him home clean," he joked.

Miley hugged her dad. She couldn't wait to go back home, take off her Hannah wig, and kick back. Just like any other normal girl with a credit card that never, *ever* came out of the third slot of a wallet. Except for emergencies.

Put your hands together
for the next Hannah
Montana book . . .

True Blue

Adapted by Laurie McElroy

Based on the series created by Michael Poryes and Rich Correll & Barry O'Brien

Based on the episode, "Cuffs Will Keep Us Together," Written by Steven Peterman

Miley Stewart and Lilly Truscott were dressed for their gym class and stretching out on the high school athletic field. Miley was already dreading what was in store. "I hate flag football," she complained. "It's just one more sport where I get picked last. And you want to know why?"

Lilly snorted. "'Cause you stink?"

Miley glared at her.

"Or, 'cause you're pretty and all the other girls are jealous?" Lilly asked in a singsong voice with a sweet smile.

"Nice save," Miley said sarcastically. "Look, I know I'm not good, but I'm not horrible."

Just then their gym teacher, Mrs McDermott, walked across the field. "Look alive, Stewart," she said, tossing Miley the football.

Instead of catching the ball, Miley threw her hands up to protect herself and tried to jump out of the way. But she didn't even do that right – the ball hit her in the head.

Lilly gave her friend a knowing look.

"Okay, I'm horrible," Miley admitted. "But you don't know how it feels always being the last one picked because nobody wants 'Stinky Stewart.'"

"Hey, last year in football I wasn't picked until practically the end," Lilly answered, trying to sympathize. But she couldn't really relate. Lilly was a great athlete.

"You had a broken collarbone," Miley reminded her. "And you still got picked ahead of me! I just wish one time some miracle would happen, and I wouldn't get picked last."

Mrs McDermott crossed the field again. She pointed to a tough-looking girl named Joannie Palumbo and then to Lilly. "Palumbo. Truscott. You're captains. Pick your teams!"

"Yes!" Miley clapped her hands excitedly. "Yes! Yes!" she cried, throwing her arms around Lilly. "Finally a captain who'll pick me first!"

Joannie Palumbo leaned in. "Doesn't matter who you pick, Truscott," she said with a hiss. "Your team is going down."

Lilly planted her hands on her hips and narrowed her eyes. She and Joannie Palumbo had been rivals since elementary school. "In your dreams, Palumbo."

Hi, I'm Hannah Montana!

One of the most awesome things about being a popstar is going on tour. It's cool getting out and meeting all the fans, plus I get to travel the world and see all kinds of smokin' places. And there's nothing better than performing to a crowd of thousands who are all totally psyched to see you.

When I was younger, all I wanted to do was share my music with others, and now that wish has come true. Whenever I'm about to go on stage, and I'm buzzin' with nerves, adrenaline and excitement, I have to pinch myself to remember it's not just a dream. Crazy and unbelievable as it is, this is actually my real life, and I'm the luckiest girl in the world!

Loads of love,

Hannah xx

xxx

Hannah's World Tour Diary

JUNE 1ST

Wow, school's out for the summer, and I'm off on my world tour! I'm so excited, I can't wait. I'm going to see so many amazing places and visit heaps of different countries that I've only ever read about until now.

I'm writing this as we're flying in first class to Europe. Our first stop is London, then we're going to Paris. We've got so much luggage with us – I need a lot of clothes for the tour, as we've got so many costume changes to do. Dad's face was hilarious when he saw how many suitcases I had!

When we arrive in London, I've got a day or two to get acclimatized (jet lag – ugh!) and then the promotional stuff starts.

Hannah's World Tour Diary

JUNE 17TH

The concerts have been going sooooo well so far! I'm really pleased, the reaction I've been getting from the crowds is just awesome. Everyone in the crowd knows the words, and they're singing along with me as I'm performing. There's nothing like hearing thousands of people singing along to lyrics you've written while your're performing. It's the best feeling in the world!

We've left Europe, and I'm living it up in Asia, which is so kickin'! We've been to Singapore already and I'm now in Hong Kong. It's a totally different culture to what I'm used to but, so far, I'm loving every minute. There's great shopping here, and some of the best food I've ever eaten. It's a good job I'm doing so much dancing at the moment, to burn off all those noodles!

This week I've got tons of interviews lined up with different TV stations, radio shows and magazines. I'm also going to be doing signings in record shops. It's all really good fun. I love meeting new people.

Hannah's World Tour Diary

JULY 2ND

Whew! Now I'm in Australia, and have just come off stage after doing my opening night in Sydney. I'm in the car with Dad, heading back to the hotel. It's the best place I've ever stayed – I'm in the presidential suite, and it's just awesome! There's a big jacuzzi bath, a view over Sydney harbour, and every night I get chocolates left on my pillow. I could seriously move into the place!

Reviews of the shows so far have been great. Everyone seems to be enjoying them and the feedback has been rockin', which makes me feel so psyched. We have all worked so hard to make sure the concerts are fabulous, and I totally feel like we've succeeded. I met some fans backstage tonight and it was kickin' to get their feedback. They said they'd had a great time, and loved the new album!

Hannah's World Tour Diary

JULY 20TH

I can't believe the end of the tour is here already. It's gone by so quickly. Lately it's felt like I've spent more time in the air than on the ground – I've been flying A LOT. But now we're back in America, which is so exciting. I've really missed hanging out with Lilly and Oliver, and I've even missed Jackson a bit, (but there's no way in the world that I'd ever tell him that!).

I've bought tons of souvenirs home with me, and have done SO much shopping. I think I have a whole closet's worth of new clothes. We're heading back to California via New York, which is where I'm performing tomorrow, then Chicago and Tennessee. I can't wait to do the Tennessee show, it's so cool going back to the South and reconnecting with my roots. Then, before I know it, I'll be back at home. I'll be ordinary girl Miley Stewart again – although writing my 'What I did over my summer vacation' report should be interesting!

HAPPENIN' CITY GUIDE FROM HANNAH

Although I spend a lot of time working while I'm on tour, a girl's still gotta have some fun! I've been to all sorts of cool places as I've travelled the world as Hannah Montana. Here's my guide to the things I've enjoyed the most in my favourite cities...

NEW YORK

What to do: I like to check out the awesome museums and galleries, walk through Central Park and take a ride on the Staten Island ferry.

What to see: I love the view from the top of the Empire State Building, taking in a basketball game and catching a show on Broadway!

What to eat: New York is just food heaven for a teenage girl like me! You can enjoy yummy pretzels, the best pizza in the world and delish cupcakes. Just don't eat too much of it – remember to keep your diet balanced, guys!

What to buy: What's not to buy in New York? There are the best clothes shops are here, plus the biggest music stores – which for me means retail paradise!

Souvenirs to take home: I found a hilarious Statue of Liberty crown for Lilly, a model of the Empire State Building for Jackson, an I LOVE NY tee for Oliver and an umbrella with the Manhattan skyline on it for Dad.

Hannah's Happenin' Cities

PARIS

What to do: I love wandering around the quirky French markets, taking a boat trip down the Seine and checking out the Champs Elysees.

What to see: The view from the top of the Eiffel Tower is breathtaking, and don't forget to enjoy the amazing art galleries, so you can pay a visit to the famous Mona.

What to eat: Oh la, la, I just adore le French food! Croque Monsieurs, tasty filled baguettes and the most delicious cheeses I've ever had. The French know how to do seriously yummy munchies.

What to buy: Paris is filled with the most amazing designer stores, you could window shop for days and not get bored! Away from the boulevards there are loads of flea markets where you can buy pretty much anything you've ever wanted at great prices.

Souvenirs to take home: I found a sassy beret for Lilly, a replica Eiffel Tower for Jackson, a caricature drawn by a street artist for Oliver and a box of French chocolates for Dad.

Hannah's Happenin' Cities

SYDNEY

What to do: I enjoy boat trips around the harbour, chilling out on the beautiful beaches and climbing Sydney Harbour Bridge (although I wouldn't recommend this if you're scared of heights!).

What to see: You have to check out the awesome and iconic Sydney Opera House, head out of town to the Blue Mountains and watch the cute surfers at Bondi Beach.

What to eat: Grab some yummy noodles in China town. If you're feeling brave, try some traditional bush tucker. I stayed away from that though – no way am I eating bugs!

What to buy: Sydney's great for shopping, so check out the malls for an awesome selection of clothes – especially sassy beachwear.

Souvenirs to take home: I found a cute cuddly kangaroo for Lilly, a traditional hat with corks for Jackson, a boomerang for Oliver and a didgeridoo for Dad.

Hannah's Happenin' Cities

LONDON

What to do: I grabbed my dancers and we took a double-decker bus tour around the city to check-out the famous landmarks, then got driven around in a traditional black cab and saw a show in the West End.

What to see: I loved Buckingham Palace, the Houses of Parliament and Tower Bridge – there's so much history here!

What to eat: Afternoon tea with scones and tiny sandwiches. For dinner we ate traditional fish and chips. Mmmmm!.

What to buy: You can pick up anything and everything in London! I hit some of the huge shops on Oxford Street to find some new clothes for the tour, then picked up several pairs of kickin' sneakers at Camden Market.

Souvenirs to take home: I found a cute tee with a Union Jack flag on for Lilly, a black taxi keyring for Jackson, a model red double-decker bus for Oliver and a magnet of Buckingham Palace for Dad.

Life on the tour bus

HOME, SWEET BUS!

Whenever I'm touring the States or Europe, I travel between cities on my super comfy tour bus. It's absolutely huge, with bedrooms, a lounge and a kitchen. It's nearly as big as my house back home – only this home's on wheels. It has everything you'd want while you're on the road.

I often chill out in the lounge with my guitar when we're travelling. It's usually miles between each venue, so the journeys can take several days sometimes. Playing the guitar and writing lyrics helps the time to go faster.

I always make sure I've got tons of my stuff around the place to make it feel more like home. I've got books, magazines, comfy cushions, shells from the beach, plus tons of photos of Dad, Jackson, Lilly and Oliver everywhere. And of course, I always have my guitar with me – I'd be totally lost without that!

Life on the tour bus

Dad's hung up some of the awards I've won around the bus. It's a great confidence booster to see them all around the world – I still get nervous before I go on stage, even after all the practise I've had at performing.

It's not easy fitting my clothes into the tiny wardrobe on the bus. I have a heap of costumes that I wear on stage, plus different outfits for all the interviews and TV appearances I have to do. I end up stealing Dad's wardrobe space!

The bus has all kinds of cool gadgets on board. There's a giant TV hidden in the cupboard, and a huge library of DVDs so we can kick back and watch movies while we're driving. The sofas fold out into giant beds, which make the lounge a perfect chill-out palace.

Dad keeps a giant scrapbook of all the reviews I've had which I often flick through when we're travelling. It keeps me focused and it's totally inspiring to read all the nice greatthings people have written about me.

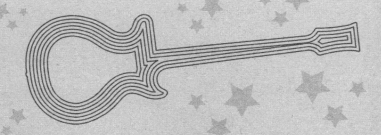

Life on the tour bus

HOME, SWEET BUS!

While I'm on the tour bus, it's really important to keep fit and healthy. It would be super easy to just pig out on junk food while I'm sitting around all day, but I know I can't do that. I need to eat well to make sure I've got enough energy to do all my dance routines. It's also important to exercise regularly, stick to a regular beauty routine and get plenty of zeds. I've got these top tips stuck to the fridge in the kitchen, so they're always at the front of my mind.

Hannah's Top Healthy Eating Tips:

 Always make sure you've got plenty of healthy, delicious food around you. This way, when the snack attack hits, you won't be tempted by chocolate and crisps.

 Remember that you can still eat things you like, just don't eat them all day, every day. Everything in moderation, that's the best way.

Hannah's Top Keep Fit Tips:

 Get exercise as often as you can. When I'm on tour, it's not always easy to exercise on the bus as there's just not enough space. Luckily, I practise my dance routines on stage a lot, which keeps me in shape.

 Stick on your favourite CD and bounce around like crazy to it. Instant exercise – and fun, too!

Hannah's Top Beauty Tips:

 Drink tons of water. It's great for your body, and helps keep your skin clear.

 Emphasize your best features. So if you have beautiful eyes, concentrate on great eye make-up.

Tour Quiz

WHAT IS YOUR DREAM CONCERT?

If you were a superstar singer, what kind of show would you put on for your fans? Take this fun quiz to find out!

 Q1 Pick your favourite music style:

A: Lots of loud guitars and drums.

B: Catchy tunes you can dance along to.

C: Bubbly, bouncy songs with an infectious chorus.

 Q2 What's your ideal outfit to perform in?

A: A sassy mini and customized tee with killer heels.

B: A gingham skirt and jeans, teamed with cowboy boots.

C: A cute dress with sneakers.

 Q3 If you were going to write a song, what would it be like?

A: Brooding and meaningful.

B: Easy to sing-along to, with an infectious beat.

C: Fun with a touch of cheekiness.

Tour Quiz

 Q1 Where would your ideal concert location be?

A: New York, New York – you love the city vibe.

B: Nashville, Tennessee – the homely South is where it's at.

C: Los Angeles, California – sun, surf and lots of fun.

 Q2 What kind of makeup would you wear on stage?

A: Lots of dark eyeliner and lipstick –
you want to make an impact.

B: Clear mascara and a touch of gloss –
you like to keep it natural.

C: Pastel eyeshadows with pink lipsticks –
you love to look girly.

 Q3 How would your audience dance
along to your music?

A: Jumping up and down with gusto.

B: Line dancing in a perfectly
synchronized routine.

C: Bouncing around and having tons
of fun.

Tour Quiz

ANSWERS!

⭐ **Mostly As:**   Your perfect show to perform at is a ROCK concert.

You have a definite flair for the dramatic and your ideal venue would be a huge auditorium. You'll play your songs at full blast, and you firmly believe you can't have too many loud guitars and crashing drums!

⭐ **Mostly Bs:**   Your perfect show to perform at is a COUNTRY concert.

You rate all things Southern, and would be just as at home performing to an intimate crowd in a barn as a concert arena. You love to join in with the line-dancing and adore a good hoedown!

Mostly Cs: Your perfect show to perform at is a POP concert.

You like fun music you can bounce around to and your concerts will reflect this. Everyone's welcome to your shows, you're very friendly and approachable and your audiences will love you for it as they sing happily along.

Coolest Hannah Quotes

Check out these cool quotes from Hannah and her friends...

 "Guess which famous popstar is going to play Zaronda, Princess of the Undead, on Zombie High?"
- Miley to Lilly.

 "When my goldfish died, my mum flushed it down the toilet. I'll never forget her comforting words: 'Get over it, Oliver, it's a stinking fish.'"
- Oliver to Miley and Lilly.

 "That's it. He crossed the line. He insulted my hair."
- Robby Stewart, after his neighbour is rude to him.

 Robbie (holding a fish): "Look at the size of this bad boy. We had quite a battle or two. First it was him, then it was me, then it was him, then it was me." Jackson: "Dad, you got it at the fish market."

 "Your grandma's in the car alone, and sooner or later she's gonna sniff out those pork scratchings I've got hidden under the seat."
- Robby to Miley

 "I know how much you love music, so I brought you aeroplane headphones!"
-Mam'aw to Miley, after she forgets to bring her a present.